Stone Arch Books
a Capstone Imprint

Benji Franklin: Kid Zillionaire
is published by Stone Arch Books,
a Capstone Imprint
1710 Roe Crest Drive
North Mankato, Minnesota 56003
www.capstoneyoungreaders.com

Cataloging-in-Publication Data is available on
the Library of Congress website.
ISBN: 978-1-4342-6419-0

Summary: After inventing a bestselling computer app,
twelve-year-old Benjamin "Benji" Franklin becomes the
world's youngest and, well, only ZILLIONAIRE. But this
tiny tycoon quickly discovers that life isn't all about
the Benjamin. He decides to use his newfound wealth
for greater good—like saving the world from killer
dinos and building superpowered rocket ships!

Graphic Designer: Brann Garvey
Creative Director: Heather Kindseth
Production Specialist: Laura Manthe

Printed in the United States of America in Stevens Point, Wisconsin.
022014   008033

BENJI FRANKLIN

KID ZILLIONAIRE

FRANKLIN

written by
Raymond Bean

illustrated by
Matthew Vimislik

CHAPTER 1
Mega-Sized Dreams

My name's Benjamin Franklin, but most people call me Benji. As you probably guessed, my parents named me after one of the most creative minds in history. Talk about pressure!

Benjamin Franklin

Benji Franklin

Brilliant

Kid

Right from the get-go, people had mega-sized dreams for me. Not to brag, but I didn't disappoint. At six months old, I learned sign language. When I was three, I taught myself how to play the guitar—acoustic, of course. At five, I was able to read in six different languages, including Dolphin (*EE-EEEK!*).

My mom thinks I'm brilliant, but I'm not so sure. Do true geniuses crave candy 24 hours a day?

A real genius, Albert Einstein, once said: "It's not that I'm so smart, it's just that I stay with problems longer." I feel the same way. It's not that I'm supersmart. I'm just really, REALLY curious!

Luckily, my dad and I share a ginormous workshop behind my house. It's a great place to create (...or break!) all kinds of stuff.

My grandpa built the workshop like a hundred years ago. Loads of his old cars, dusty boats, rusty motors, and other odd items still fill the rotting shed. If it flew, rolled, or floated, there's a good chance it's hiding in there somewhere.

My dad grew up tinkering with stuff, too. In fact, he's so good at building things that last year he created a satellite from a car radio, a spare tire, an aquarium, and the rear seat of a minivan.

A few weeks ago, we launched the satellite into space from our backyard. It. Was. AWESOME!

Minivan Seat

Aquarium

Spare Tire

Earth

Car Radio

Kids at school didn't believe me when I told them about the satellite...until I showed them the FBI footage. (Don't ask!)

One day, while I downloaded data from the satellite, my dad rolled up on his rusty old motorcycle. "Your piano lesson starts in ten minutes," he said, taking off his helmet.

"But I'm tracking asteroids," I replied. "There's dozens of them whizzing by today!"

Dad walked over and peeked at the data. "How's the satellite looking?" he asked, adjusting his glasses.

"It'll be fine," I assured him. "It doesn't seem like any of the 'roids will take it out."

"That's good news," he said, opening the workshop door. "Because I have work to do!"

After reading a news article about a fisherman who fell overboard, Dad towed an old boat into our workshop. Then he started designing a safety system for fishing boats. His idea was to cover each crewmember's jacket, pants, and boots with thousands of tiny magnets and rig the fishing boat with a superpowered magnet. If a fisherman fell in the water, the magnet could pull him back to the boat safely.

"How's the suit coming?" I asked.

"I'm ready for a test, Benji," he said, putting on one of the magnetic jackets. "Climb into the boat with me, will you? Let's see if this gizmo is strong enough to pull me back in!"

"Are you sure it's safe to test?" I asked.

"Nope! But there's only one way to find out." Dad leaped off the boat and onto the shed floor below. "Man overboard!" he cried out.

I flipped the safety switch. Instead of being pulled toward the ship, he shot away from it as if he'd been fired out of a cannon. **WHAM!!** He blasted through the old shed like a human wrecking ball.

I quickly jumped off the boat and ran up to the hole in the wall.

"Are you all right, Dad?" I asked, worried.

"Yep! Guess I had the magnets reversed," he said. "When you flipped the switch, they repelled instead of attracted me. If the attraction is that strong, I think this idea just might work, son."

"Benji! Your piano teacher is here!" I heard Mom shout from the house.

"Do I have to go, Dad?" I asked.

"You know the drill, kiddo. Piano is great for the mind," he said. "It helps develop your synapses."

"What if my synapses don't want developing?"

"As much as I'd like for you to stay here and give me a hand, you've got to go," he replied.

"But...what if I had a terrible headache?" I asked, holding my forehead.

"You'd have to go straight to bed and maybe the doctor," he said.

"But...what if—" I began.

"Benji, what if you stopped trying to excuse yourself?" he said. "Go tickle those ivories."

CHAPTER 2
Excuse Yourself

Weeks earlier, my tech teacher, Mrs. Heart, had assigned a class project. Each student in the class had to create a computer app that people would want to buy.

When Dad said, "What if you stopped trying to excuse yourself?," an idea hit me like an asteroid. Kids all over the world try getting out of BORING stuff every day. They make up endless excuses to avoid the chores they don't want to do.

What if I created an app to help kids get out of these tasks? I wondered. *Like piano lessons!*

I even thought of an app name...Excuse Yourself!

I could hardly concentrate during my piano lesson. I kept thinking about my grandfather. He used to say that his greatest ideas always came to him in a flash.

"Brilliance strikes like lightning!" he'd tell me. "One minute it's not there, and the next—**BOOM!**—an idea flashes across the sky. You can't miss it."

The Excuse Yourself computer app was a brilliant idea. I knew that much instantly.

After a few days, the app worked just the way I wanted it. I'd taught myself how to write computer code when I was younger, and the skill really came in handy. Mrs. Heart had taught us a few useful tricks in class to help create an app, but most of the cooler features I had figured out on my own.

The day the app was due, I realized most of the kids in my class had created *games*. As my time to present neared, I could hardly contain my excitement. A few kids presented before me, and then Mrs. Heart called me to the front of the class.

I stood in front of the large digital board. "How many of you have made up an excuse to get yourself out of trouble?" I asked.

Every hand went up. *Perfect!* I thought.

"Of course you have," I continued. "We all make excuses, and even lie from time to time. But what if I told you there was an app that helps you get out of trouble? Raise your hand if you'd use it."

Again, every hand went up.

This time though, when the hands went back down, one person's remained up—Cindy Meyers's.

Cindy never raised her hand unless she wanted to complain about something. "Do you want to say something, Cindy?" I asked, cautiously.

"If you're talking about an excuse app, Benji, save your breath," she said. "It's been done." She pointed to another app on her cellphone.

"You're right," I agreed. "Plenty of excuse apps already exist, but none like the one I've created!"

I tapped the digital board, and my computer app launched. The words "Excuse Yourself" appeared on the screen's homepage.

"Clever name, Benji!" the teacher exclaimed.

"Thanks, Mrs. Heart," I said. "Like it's name, the Excuse Yourself app is anything but ordinary. If you need an excuse, simply type your question into the powerful search engine." I scrolled through the app's menu bar, demonstrating for the class.

"Like other apps, Excuse Yourself gives you dozens of possible excuses," I explained. "But, unlike the competition, my computer app helps you determine the likelihood the excuse will work! Someone give me an example of something you needed an excuse for today."

A kid named Mark raised his hand. "I got in trouble last period," he said. "I didn't read the book Mr. Frayne assigned."

"Fantastic!" I said. Then I typed: **Didn't read the book I was supposed to read for class.**

The app immediately created a list of excuses:

EXCUSE	ODDS OF WORKING
Lost it.	**30%**
Family emergency.	**85%**
Book made me cry.	**80%**
Read the book; couldn't understand it.	**67%**
Received eye drops at doctor; can't see.	**98%**
Headache/stomachache/ache of any kind.	**25%**

More options...

The class seemed interested.

"That's not all," I continued. "Once I've made my selection, the app will advise me of the possible challenges I may encounter if I decide to use this excuse. Which one do you want to use, Mark?"

"The eye drops," he replied. "That's a new one."

I clicked on the fifth option: **Received eye drops at doctor; can't see.**

The app generated a list of advice for the user:

· **May need a note.**

· **School nurse may call or e-mail home to confirm.**

· **Teacher may ask, "What's wrong?" Say you don't know the name of the condition; a kid wouldn't remember something like that.**

· **Rub your eyes, but don't overdo it.**

"That's awesome!" Mark said.

"Hold on. The app goes one step further, " I said. "Most kids use the same excuse over and over. I've added a feature that tracks when you've used excuses and who you've used them on." Again, I demonstrated the feature on screen.

"Also, the app keeps a record of all your excuse activity," I explained. "If someone asks you about an excuse you gave a few weeks back, there's no need to remember the details. Simply click your excuse history, and it's all there for you."

You could've heard a pin drop in the classroom. The other students' minds were spinning with possibilities. My teacher chewed her bottom lip and tried to force a smile.

A few kids had their cell phones out. They were hiding them under the desks, so Mrs. Heart wouldn't notice. I thought it was pretty rude that they were playing on their phones, and I hadn't even finished my presentation!

Mrs. Heart interrupted. "I just want to be clear, Benji. Are you encouraging kids to lie?"

"No, ma'am!" I exclaimed. "Honesty is the best policy, of course. I'm saying that, like it or not, we all tell fibs from time to time. My Excuse Yourself app helps once someone has already made the decision to make an excuse."

"That stills sounds a lot like lying," she said.

"Kids already do a lot of lying on their own," I argued. "And that brings me to one final feature, which I'm very proud of."

I felt like a salesman on a TV infomercial. I was really selling it! "Excuse Yourself provides users with graphs, data, and charts to help them understand how often they make excuses," I explained. "Kids might actually learn about their behavior and maybe even change." Mrs. Heart had to like that part, even though she was unsure about the app.

"Very imaginative," said Mrs. Heart. "I just wanted to make sure you weren't encouraging lying in order to get out of responsibility."

"It's AWESOME, Franklin!" Mark said again.

"Yes, Mark," Mrs. Heart said. "It is awesome, but it still concerns me a bit. You kids shouldn't actually use the Excuse Yourself app. It's simply a fun idea."

"Can I buy it?" asked Mark, ignoring her.

"It's available online," I replied. "But, like Mrs. Heart said, the app's not really for everyday use. It's more of a goof than anything else."

$ $ $

That night, I helped Dad in the workshop with the deep-sea safety gear. The magnets were working much better. When he flipped the switch, the magnets pulled me across the floor. The invention wasn't ready to pull a grown man out of the ocean, but it was getting closer.

After that, we tracked some debris approaching our satellite, and then we headed to pick Mom up from the food pantry where she volunteers.

When we arrived, she was organizing cans of food and placing them on shelves.

"I'm about ready to go," she said. "I just want to drop a care package off to a family on the way."

"No problem," Dad said.

She grabbed me by the hand. "Come with me, Benjamin. You can help carry a few more things."

Mom has volunteered at the food pantry so long that she practically runs the place. She handed me an empty bag and walked toward the fridges.

"Grab two containers of milk and some butter," she said to me. "I'll meet you back at the front."

I opened the large, silver refrigerator doors and walked inside. It was FREEZING! I saw some chicken, eggs, and butter, but no milk. I grabbed the items and headed back to the front to meet Mom.

"You're out of milk," I told her.

"Again?" she said with a sigh. "I can't seem to keep it on the shelves. We'll have to stop on the way and pick some up."

"We'd better go," Dad said. "It looks like rain."

"Please tell me you didn't bring that ridiculous motorcycle," Mom groaned.

"I didn't bring that *ridiculous* motorcycle," Dad said, smirking. He turned to me and whispered, "It's not ridiculous."

"Uh-huh," Mom said. "Then I'm driving. Benji, you can sit in the sidecar with your father."

"Not AGAIN!" Dad cried.

Dad got funny looks from people when he drove the motorcycle. But when Mom was driving with Dad and me in the sidecar...people died laughing!

$ $ $

We stopped to buy milk and then dropped the supplies off for a family. I was surprised that there were two kids playing out in front of the house when we pulled up. I'd been to the pantry with Mom many times, but I'd never seen the families she helped in person. The mother hugged my mom. It was clear that Mom had been there many times before. She introduced us to the woman and her kids.

"Your mother is one of the most generous people I've ever known," said the woman.

"I just like to help," said Mom.

"You're an amazing person," the woman added.

"You guys take care of yourselves," Mom told them. "Remember, let me know if you need anything at all."

The woman teared up as we left. I never knew how much Mom's work helped people.

Later that night, I was setting the table for dinner. "How would those people have fed their kids if you didn't bring them all that stuff?" I asked.

"I'm not sure, Benji," she replied.

"How come you guys were out of milk?" I asked.

"We operate on donations, so we only have what people give us," Mom explained. "Today, there wasn't enough milk, so I decided to buy it."

"How often do you buy the stuff yourself?"

"More often than you'd think," she said. "We get a bunch of food around the holidays, but the rest of the year is pretty tough. Working on donations alone just isn't sustainable. We're always running out of things and people go hungry."

"Isn't there a better way to help people that need food?" I said.

"When you figure it out," she said. "I'm all ears."

CHAPTER 3

My First Million

The next morning was Saturday. I logged into the bank account I'd created for my app. I figured a few kids in my class might have bought it. Maybe I'd have enough money to buy some candy (YUM!).

I clicked my balance and couldn't believe my eyes! When I left for school Friday, my account was at $1.39 because I'd bought the app myself to make

sure it worked. The app sold for $1.99 online. Every time someone bought it, $1.39 went straight to my new bank account.

I was expecting ten dollars or so, but the balance was...$344,052!

CHA-CHING!!

I got out my calculator and divided the balance by $1.39. If my math was correct (and why wouldn't it be!), the app had been downloaded nearly 250,000 times. Overnight!

This must be a mistake, I thought. I refreshed the page, expecting the number to return to something like ten cents. But instead...

$353,060!

CHA-CHING!!

Could that many people have downloaded the app in only a few seconds? I clicked it a third time, and the number went up again!

By the time I called my parents into my room, the account was even higher. The numbers were changing so rapidly that it reminded me of numbers on the gas pump when Dad fills the tank. They were spinning too fast to even make out the digits.

"You didn't hack into a bank or anything, did you?" Dad asked, warily.

"Of course he didn't hack into a bank. Don't be ridiculous," Mom said. "You didn't, did you?"

"No!"

"The Federal Reserve?" Dad asked.

"Remember that computer app I created for tech class?" I asked.

"The last time you mentioned it, you were stuck for ideas," Dad replied.

"Right! But I got an idea when I was trying to get out of my piano lesson the other day," I explained. "I built an app and presented it to the class yesterday. I put it up for sale on the app store, but I didn't expect people to actually buy it."

"This is all from a computer app?" Mom asked. "How can you make this much selling an app?"

"It's going viral!" Dad exclaimed, sitting at my desk to have a closer look at the data.

"This thing is being downloaded all over the world," he said. "What does it do, Benji?"

Net
Income:
$575,359

"It makes excuses," I said, anticipating a reaction from my mom.

"Why doesn't the number stop spinning?" Mom asked. "It just keeps getting bigger."

"Because it's being downloaded so often," Dad said. "Every time someone buys the app, the number goes up. This is amazing! I've never seen anything like it."

"What does this thing do again?" Mom asked.

"It's called Excuse Yourself," I repeated softly.

"How wonderful!" said Mom, giving me a big smile. "So it teaches young people good manners?"

"Uh...not exactly," I said.

She gave me a stony stare. "You better show me how it works."

$ $ $

When Mom downloaded the app to her phone, she clicked around silently for a few minutes. She didn't look too happy.

"I'm not sure this is appropriate, Benjamin," she said. "All these people are using your app to get out of trouble. They're lying!"

"They're not really lying, Mom," I assured her.

"Actually, they are," she said. "You've given people a way of getting out of responsibilities in a dishonest way. Last time I checked, *that* was lying."

"People lie all the time, Mom," I said. "They don't ever really think about how often they're doing it. Maybe it will help people see the amount of excuses they're making and change?"

"Nice try, kiddo," she said. "Why couldn't you have created something more useful and positive?"

"Mrs. Heart told us we had to create an app that people would want to buy," I replied. "I didn't expect it to go beyond my classroom."

"Hmmm."

"I was just having fun with it, Mom," I added. "Who would have thought it would be this popular?"

"Hey, check this out!" Dad interrupted. "Benji's app is being discussed all over the Internet."

He was right.

The app *had* gone viral.

Bloggers and websites all over the globe were writing about it. Some people were saying how great it was. Others were really angry about the idea.

We silently read several of the articles and tried to grasp what was happening.

"I think we should have breakfast and give this a little time to process," Dad said. "I haven't even had a chance to look at this miraculous new creation."

We all sat at the kitchen table. Mom and Dad each played with Excuse Yourself. After several moments of silence, Dad said, "I won't be able to mow the lawn this weekend because I'm suffering from seasonal allergies."

"You don't have allergies!" Mom said, focusing on the app.

"Then, I can't mow the lawn because I twisted my ankle yesterday," he said, giving me a wink. "It still feels a little tender."

Mom picked up on what he was doing. "Very cute, honey," she said. "Your ankle is fine, and I wish I could say the same for your son's app."

"I think it's interesting," Dad said, hesitantly.

"And inappropriate," Mom added.

"I don't know if I'd say 'inappropriate,'" Dad responded. "But it's definitely controversial."

"Our son has basically created a database of lies people can use to get out of work," she said.

"True, but it's up to the individual to decide if they're going to use an excuse or not." Dad continued to defend me. "Once they click on the site, they've already made the decision to find an excuse. Benji didn't have anything to do with that."

Dad held his bowl of cereal in the air. "A chef can't be blamed for the customer's hunger," he said.

Dad added, "The customer is already hungry. The chef only provides the food."

"Benji isn't cooking *food*," said Mom. He's cooking up *lies*. We've got a real problem here."

"Guys," I interrupted.

"Yes?" Mom asked, annoyed.

"I'm sorry to interrupt," I said, "but I might have just become a MILLIONAIRE!!"

CHAPTER 4
Zillionaire?

The week that followed was *completely* insane! Every news show, magazine, blog, and tech company wanted to meet me. One company even offered me a job, but we would've had to move to California, and Dad has a fear of earthquakes.

I couldn't believe they'd offered a kid my age a job. My parents and I did interviews, took phone calls, and tried our best to manage all the attention.

My parents were most excited for all the interviews and talk shows. Especially the interview with the news show *Your World with Chuck Matthews*. They watch it every Sunday night and were thrilled to be on the show. We did the interview on Saturday afternoon. It was on that show's interview that Mom's concerns about honesty were really put to the test.

"Are you worried that your son, Benji, has created an app that helps people lie?" Chuck Matthews asked Mom.

Mom froze, but just for a nanosecond. "Well, Mr. Matthews, that's a question Benjamin and I have discussed a great deal," she replied. "We're hopeful that Excuse Yourself is a place where people—"

"What are your plans for the money your son is making?" interrupted Chuck Matthews.

"We're adjusting to it," said Dad. "For now, life for Benjamin will remain the same as it always—"

"I hear you have a golden submarine," said Chuck, turning to me.

"Two of them, actually," I replied. "The first one sank, so I had to buy a second one to go down and rescue the crew."

"And you have a private island?" asked Chuck.

I waved my hand. "Just a small one, Chuck," I said. "Although I have applied for nation status."

My mom tried to change the subject. "Uh, we feel the app is a good way for Benjamin to connect with the world," she said.

"Yes," chimed in Dad. "It's a way to connect more positively and—"

"What's this I hear about a space station?" asked Chuck, looking directly at me.

"Space is where it's at, Chuck," I said. "And it's a great place to keep my zoo."

Benji Franklin
"Kid Zillionaire"

"Your zoo?" he said.

"I was running out of room on the island," I said. "Those Tibetan yaks take up a lot more room than you'd think."

"You have yaks?" asked Chuck.

"For the milk," I said. "It's very healthy."

Then Chuck stared out at his studio audience and said, "I bet I'd like some of that. You know how much I like to *yak*!"

The audience went wild. They cheered and laughed and even clapped.

Chuck sat back in his chair and smiled at me. I could tell the interview was going well. "So," he said at last, "you're a sixth-grade zillionaire?"

"A zillion isn't a real number," I pointed out.

"True," said Chuck, nodding. "But what else do you call a kid with more money than he can count?"

"Generous," said my mother quickly.

"Thoughtful," said my father.

"Lucky," I said. "And very excited about my new space station."

CHAPTER 5
Greater Good

The next morning, we got a mysterious call from a man named Dr. Snow. Dad talked to him for a while, and then he handed me the phone. I figured it was another interview, or another celebrity, or another pro athlete who wanted to hang out.

"Hi, Benji," a voice on the other end said. "I'm a researcher and founder of the B.A.D.R. Institute. I've been following your story. We have a situation here at the Institute that we feel you might be able to assist with. Are you free to come out and meet us tomorrow night?"

"Hmm, I don't know," I said. "Where are you located? Can I get there by nuclear sub?"

"Uh, no."

"Can I get there by solar-powered rocket ship?"

"No."

"Can I get there by dogsled pulled by twelve Olympic athletes?" (I can pay for all those things, by the way.)

"No."

"Wow!" I said. "You guys must be hidden in some supersecret faraway exotic location!"

"We're fifteen miles down the road," he said.

"Oh," I said.

"Our situation is rather dire," said the man. "We need to meet in person."

"I'm a kid," I explained, although I'm sure he already knew. "I have school. Which is also dire. You'll have to work out the details with my dad."

I yawned and handed the phone to Dad, and he walked off with it.

Saying "I'm a kid" is an excuse that I came up with on my app. It works in almost every situation with adults.

"What was that all about?" Mom asked.

"I don't know," I said. "They wanted to talk with me about a problem they have."

"I think this app is just the beginning of big things for you, Benjamin," she said. "Promise me you won't lose sight of who you are."

"I promise," I assured her. "Nothing has really changed if you think about it. Well, maybe my clothes. And the private island and stuff. Otherwise, all that's happened is a bunch of people are downloading the app."

"When things settle down, we'll have to sort out what we're going to do with all that money," said Mom. "I hope you don't forget that it's not all about the Benjamins, Benjamin."

"What does that mean?" I asked. I couldn't help smirking a bit because Mom was trying to be cool.

"Isn't that what people call large sums of money?" she asked. "Don't they say that in movies?"

"They do," I said. "And you don't have to worry. I know it's not all about the Benjamins, Mom."

"There are things in the world that matter more than money," she said. "You saw for yourself the other day how that family was in need."

"I know, Mom."

"Did you know I read this morning about an entire town that is in need?" she said.

"How does that happen?" I asked.

"They live in a town called Shiny Desert," she explained. "It's way out in the middle of nowhere."

Mom continued. "The people who live there went for work because a big computer company built its offices out there. They wanted to develop their product in complete secrecy. These people worked there for years and, all of a sudden, the company went out of business. There's nothing else there, but the people in the town can't afford to move away."

"Can your pantry help them?" I asked.

"We've sent what we can," she said. "Other pantries are sending what they can as well, but the town is in big trouble. They're in the middle of the desert. There's nothing around for miles."

"Let's donate some of the money from Excuse Yourself to help them out," I said.

"I might just ask you to do that," she said. "For now, you just make sure the next thing you invent does more than just get people out of trouble. Think about the greater good."

The greater good? That would be a cool name for an app.

"I won't be inventing anything new for a while, Mom," I said. "Besides, I have school tomorrow!"

CHAPTER 6

B.A.D.R. Institute

Fifteen miles from my house was the site of an old airport. I'd always thought the buildings there were abandoned, but it was where the B.A.D.R. Institute was located.

Late the next night, my dad drove me out to meet Dr. Snow. "What do you think they want?" I shouted over the roar of the motorcycle.

"Who knows?" Dad said. "That scientist said he'd have to explain when we got there."

"It's a little strange that they want to meet at ten o'clock at night, don't you think?" I asked. "I researched them on the computer, and I couldn't find anything. It's a little weird."

Dad shrugged. "If it's weird, we'll leave," he said. "No biggie."

When we arrived, a security guard stood at the entrance to the facility. Dad explained who we were and who we were there to see. The guard's eye twitched a few times. He looked behind him, shining his flashlight toward the woods.

"Everything okay?" Dad asked.

"That depends," the guard replied.

"On what?" I asked.

"On your definition of 'okay,'" he replied.

"I'm not sure what you mean," Dad said.

"You will soon enough," the guard said. "Dr. Snow and the others are in building seven, all the way in the back. It's the only one with a light on."

The guard turned his attention to the woods. "They're waiting for you."

$$ \$ \, \$ \, \$ $$

When we rolled up, Dr. Snow was waiting for us outside. He was much, much, much older looking than I'd expected. Maybe TWICE as old as Dad.

"Mr. Franklin," Dr. Snow said, as I climbed out of the sidecar. I figured he was talking to my dad until he walked toward me, holding his hand out for a handshake. "Pleasure to meet you."

I shook his hand and noticed he was glancing toward the woods like the security guard.

"Come on," he said. "We'd better get inside."

Inside, a large oval table sat in the center of a massive room. The room looked like an old hangar for airplanes. It had a really high ceiling. There were about twenty people sitting around the table. They looked about the same age as Dr. Snow.

Dr. Snow introduced us to the group and asked us to have a seat.

"I have to say, this is a little strange. Benji and I are a bit confused about why we're here," Dad said.

"Understood," Dr. Snow said, clicking a button on his phone. A large screen lowered from the ceiling and the lights dimmed. "Mr. Franklin, we've been following your story. We read the articles about you and think it's amazing that a local kid is receiving so much attention for his intellect. You're clearly very creative, and we think you can help us out. Unfortunately, we find ourselves in a particularly sensitive situation."

I couldn't remember a time in my life when people were so nice to me. Kids usually gave me a hard time because I'm smart. When I was really young, sometimes I pretended to be confused in class just to fit in with the others. Something was changing though. I felt more proud of being smart and not as embarrassed.

"Who are you guys?" I asked. "I couldn't find anything online about the B.A.D.R. Institute."

"Our work is top secret and privately funded," said Dr. Snow. "Few people know what we do."

"What does your name stand for?" Dad asked.

"It stands for Bio Advancement of Dinosaur Research Institute," the scientist explained.

"Before I tell you the specifics," he continued, "I'll have to ask you sign this paper stating that you won't share any of the details we tell you tonight. We'll have to ask you to sign as well, Mr. Franklin." He turned toward my dad.

Dad nodded to me, and we both signed.

"Very well," Dr. Snow said, collecting the papers. "Do you know what a Troodon dinosaur is?"

"Hmm...didn't they star in the movie *Jurassic Park*?" I said.

"We recently obtained rare samples of Troodon DNA," he continued. "To make a long story short, we've managed to clone them."

He clicked his remote and a holographic image of a dinosaur appeared above us.

"You have living dinosaurs!" I exclaimed.

"You could say that," a woman across the larger table said. From the expression on Dr. Snow's face, I could tell he didn't like the woman very much.

"We don't have to get into all the specifics, Professor Kent," Dr. Snow said, interrupting.

"If he's going to help, doctor, he's going to need all the details. We don't have much time," Dr. Kent replied.

"How does all this involve Benji?" Dad asked.

"As I hinted on the phone last night, we have a situation," said Dr. Snow.

"Good grief! Just come out with it already," Dr. Kent shouted. "The Troodon escaped!"

"We have, um, misplaced them," Dr. Snow corrected her.

"They're out of their pens, and we haven't seen them in forty-eight hours! They're probably still in the woods behind the Institute, but there's no way to be sure," Dr. Kent added.

I was still trying to fully comprehend that they had living dinosaurs on the loose. The room was silent, and they were all looking at me.

"I'm not sure what you guys want me for," I said.

"You created Excuse Yourself. If there's anyone who can think of a way out of this situation, it's you," Dr. Snow said.

Dr. Snow seemed really worried to me in that moment. It was like he was a kid that got in trouble and couldn't get himself out. Dr. Kent acted a little like his mother (although she obviously wasn't!).

"You realize I created that app in my sixth-grade tech class?" I said. "I'm not a scientist or anything."

"Yes, but you're an expert in creating excuses," said Dr. Snow. "We need several if we're going to keep this from the public. Do you know what will happen if people learn prehistoric beasts are roaming around the city?"

"I can't imagine they'll be too happy," Dad said.

Dr. Kent added, "Benji, catching these dinosaurs isn't going to be easy. They're highly intelligent, and the land behind our facility extends for miles. If we don't catch them soon, and they make contact with people, we're going to have a much bigger problem on our hands."

Dr. Snow agreed. "We have to catch them in a way that no one knows this little mishap ever took place," he said. "We want to continue to study the Troodon in secrecy at another location. If the public learns about their existence, we'll never have peace again, and the Troodon will be doomed."

I didn't want to be rude or anything, but I had to ask. "I hope you guys don't take this the wrong way, but if you were clever enough to figure out how to clone live dinosaurs, shouldn't you be able to figure out a way to catch them without my help?"

"*We* didn't clone them, Benji," Dr. Kent shared. "Dr. Snow, who happens to be very wealthy, paid the world's leading biologists to clone the Troodon."

"Once the dinosaurs escaped," she said, "the scientists were afraid of getting in trouble, so they bailed out. They left us to clean up the mess."

"So if you hired scientists to do the work, what are you guys?" I asked.

"We're paleontologists, Benji," said Dr. Snow. "We know a lot about dinosaur bones and their history, but not a whole lot about how to handle them if they're alive."

"You're young enough to appreciate the dinosaurs, Benji," added Dr. Kent. "We're afraid that if we share our situation with adults, they'll want to capitalize on it and make money. We just want to catch the Troodon safely and continue our research, not exploit them or cause them any more harm. It's got to be you. You may be our only hope."

CHAPTER 7

The Troodon Solution

Sometimes when I'm solving a problem, my mind takes over, and I can't hear anything else around me. It happens when I solve puzzles and complex problems. My mind visualizes the solution one piece at a time. I see a bunch of different images in my head. The images swirl around in my

mind, independent of one another. If I concentrate hard enough, I can always find a way that they connect together to make a solution.

My mother says that when I was really young, I used to call this process chicken-and-idea soup!

Even today, when I get in a deep concentration while solving a problem, my parents say I'm making soup. It was happening at the table. I was completely zoned out.

I was aware that Dad and the scientist were still talking, but I was too lost in my thoughts to hear what they were saying. There were so many things running through my mind at once that it was hard to keep up. I envisioned myself capturing the Troodon and sending them somewhere safe. My mother was there. We were standing in a field, and she was really proud of me. In that moment, it all clicked.

"I see it!" I said, snapping out of my haze.

"You see the Troodon?" asked Dr. Kent, turning around quickly.

"A solution," I said. "I think I can solve your problem, but I'm going to need a few things first."

"Just like that? You've figured out a solution?" Dr. Kent asked.

"What will you need?" Dr. Snow asked.

I grabbed a pen and a sheet of paper from the table and wrote out my list. It was like a dream. I knew that if I didn't write everything down, I might forget something important:

15,000 Square feet of clear, high-security glass

1 Remote-control helicopter with video camera

1 Crew of carpenters/painters

1 Crane

1 Large flatbed truck

$6 million dollars in cash

75 –100 Dairy cows

150 –200 Chickens

I slid the note across the table to Dr. Snow. "Chickens?" he said. "You need chickens and cows?"

"We'll need them if we're going to do this right," I said. "It's not for me. It's for the greater good."

"This will be expensive," said Dr. Snow.

"Brain power isn't cheap," I said, acting confident.

"And you can guarantee that no one will learn of the Troodon?" Dr. Kent asked.

"Unless someone here tells people about it," I said, "I guarantee it."

"Can you guarantee the safety of those chickens as well?" she added.

"I'm not prepared to answer that at this point."

"Personally, I'm not so sure you've even cloned a dinosaur successfully," Dad said, challenging them a bit. "No offense, it's just I'm a man of science. I haven't seen any evidence so far to lead me to think this is a real problem you have here."

"Oh, I wish we were making this up, Mr. Franklin," Dr. Kent said. "You'll see soon enough, the Troodon are quite real."

"Well, that's what I'll need if I'm going to capture them. I can do it quickly, and no one will ever know this happened," I said. "You'll have your solution and an excuse for any commotion we might cause."

"You've got a deal," Dr. Snow said.

A younger man who'd been sitting quietly across the table said, "Let's hear how the kid plans to capture the Troodon." The lack of white in his hair meant he was the youngest one in the room, except for me of course.

"I don't want to know, Professor Clive," Dr. Snow said. "If the Troodon damage or hurt someone, it'll cost us far more than what Benji is asking. I'll order the materials right away. We'll send you a bill when the Troodon are all bolted safely back in their enclosures."

"Well, in that case, what are we sitting around here talking for?" I asked. "I don't know about you, Dad, but I want to see a living dinosaur!"

"That makes two of us," he said.

$ $ $

Young Dr. Clive insisted the other scientists wait in building seven. He took Dad and I to the hangar.

We walked for several minutes down a long, narrow trail behind the buildings that led to a clearing. "Was this the old runway when this place was an airport?" I asked, glancing out into the darkness.

"Yep," Dr. Clive replied, pointing at an old airplane hangar on the far side of the clearing. The farther we walked, I could hear a high-pitched screeching.

"Is that—?" I started to ask.

"Yes, Benji," he replied. "That is the sound of a living dinosaur."

Inside the hangar, there was only a three-foot wide space to stand in. The rest of the room was enclosed in a glass cage that rose all the way to the ceiling. "They're nocturnal, you know, so she should be pretty active," said Dr. Clive.

It was dark inside, except for the moonlight coming through the window. My eyes took a few seconds to adjust.

Dr. Clive gripped my arm and turned me toward the farthest corner of the hangar. He pointed. The Troodon stood so still that if I didn't know better I would have thought it was a statue.

The beast stood about fifteen feet from us and was a little taller than me. We were as silent as possible. I didn't even breathe. It shrieked, causing the hair on the back of my neck to stand up and my skin to tingle with excitement.

"Unbelievable!" I whispered to Dad.

"Totally," he whispered back.

"I wonder how much she'd cost," I said.

"Is that enough proof for you, Mr. Franklin?" Dr. Clive asked.

"Yes, sir," Dad and I answered at the same time.

I couldn't look away. The Troodon had a long, thin head and an even thinner neck. It reminded me of a mini *T. rex*. The skin was like a lizard's. It was muscular and stood on two legs like an ostrich.

"That's the coolest thing I've ever seen!" I said.

"It's also the most insanely dangerous thing you may ever encounter," Dr. Clive warned. "Don't take these beasts lightly, young man. They're brighter than you might imagine."

"They must be clever if they managed to get out of here," I said, looking around the enclosure.

"They had one of the largest brains in the dinosaur world," explained Dr. Clive.

"You must mean *have*," said Dad. I was wondering how to transport the Troodon to my space station zoo.

"Dr. Snow thought he'd be able to bring them back and train them to be pets."

"Looks like they outsmarted Dr. Snow," I said.

"A rock could outsmart Dr. Snow," whispered Dr. Clive. "He's book smart, but he doesn't have any common sense. I tried to warn him that this was a bad idea, but he wanted no part of it."

"He's the reason the others got out," Clive said. "*He* left the enclosure open! I don't know which I find more unbelievable: the fact that we cloned dinosaurs, or the fact that we were careless enough to let them escape."

Dad and I were hardly listening. We were both entranced by the Troodon.

"I love dinosaurs," he said. "Always have. The Troodon is miraculous. Some scientists theorize that if the dinosaurs hadn't died off, the Troodon would have evolved into a being with intelligence similar to that of humans."

"Humans?" I said.

"I've always thought they were more like birds than anything else. They just happened to have enormous brains," he said. "Now that I've actually seen them and looked them in the eye...if they'd had time to evolve another 70 million years or so, who knows? Maybe they'd be running this planet instead of us."

"Well, Dr. Clive, I think I should see one of these fellas in the wild, if I'm going to catch them," I said.

"That shouldn't be a problem. I know the perfect place," Dr. Clive said.

$ $ $

Moments later, we were waiting up in a lookout tower that Dr. Clive said was an old air signal tower, when Dad's cell phone rang. "It's Mom," he said.

Dr. Clive had already put out some meat in the field below us. He wanted to draw the Troodon out where I could see them.

Dad answered in a whisper. "Hi…I know it's late, honey," he said. "I'm not sure how much longer… you wouldn't believe me if I told you…I know he has school tomorrow…he's right here. Hold on."

I took the phone.

"Hi, Mom," I whispered.

"What are you guys doing? It's almost midnight," she asked.

"I know, Mom, but we're experiencing something that I can't really even believe is happening," I said. "I'll tell you all about it when I get home in the morning." She wasn't too happy about the fact that I was out so late, but she could tell it was important.

"Didn't you sign an agreement that you wouldn't tell anyone outside of the group about the dinosaurs?" Dr. Clive asked.

"Yes, but my mom doesn't count," I replied. "If you can't trust your mom, who can you trust?"

The Troodon appeared as if on cue. There were three of them. They gnawed on the meat and glanced cautiously around. More appeared slowly from the woods. Each one looked gray in the moonlight, stood about three feet tall, and looked like it had crawled right out of a sci-fi movie.

"That is officially the most amazing thing I've ever seen," I whispered to Dad, handing him his cell phone. He tried to take it, but must have lost his grip because it fell to the floor.

The noise startled the Troodon and, in an instant, they were gone.

"Now you see why catching them will be such a challenge," Dr. Clive said. "They're quick and smart. You've got your work cut out for you."

"Don't worry about it," I assured him. "No one will even know they were loose."

CHAPTER 8
The Daily Grind

Dad and I didn't get home until four in the morning. Still, I managed to drag myself to class.

"Someone looks tired," Mrs. Heart said, spotting me napping at my desk.

"I was up working on, uh..." I remembered my contract with the Institute. "A special project."

"You're too exhausted to learn," she said.

"I am!" I exclaimed. "In fact, I think I'd like to talk with the principal, Mrs. Heart. Can you please call down to her office and see if Mrs. Petty will meet me?"

Mrs. Heart looked shocked. She stared at me as if I had just said something in a foreign language that she didn't understand.

"What did you ask, Benji?" she said. "Are you sure you don't mean the nurse?"

"No, I'd like to see Mrs. Petty, the principal," I repeated. "Please."

"She's a busy woman, Benji," Mrs. Heart replied. "Students are usually not given the opportunity to simply stroll in and have a meeting."

"I realize that, and I mean no disrespect, Mrs. Heart," I continued. "But I'm going to need to see the principal."

The other kids were as confused as Mrs. Heart.

As far as I knew, a student at my school had never asked to sit down with the principal.

But, after a few moments, she agreed.

$ $ $

Ten minutes later, I returned to class with a note from the principal. The note informed Mrs. Heart that I was headed home early, and I'd be out for a few days. My classmates were stunned, but they weren't as shocked as my mother was when she arrived to pick me up.

"You must be so proud of Benji," the principal said to Mom, in the office.

"I'm very proud of him," Mom said, looking confused.

"First, the success of his app." Mrs. Petty was clearly working to fake a smile. "Which, I'll admit, is causing a lot of problems at the school, but at the same time raising some interesting conversations about honesty in the classroom."

"To be honest, I'm not a big fan of the app either," Mom added.

"But you must be so proud of his newest project!" Mrs. Petty exclaimed.

"I am," Mom said, looking confused. I knew Dad had told her about the Troodon after I left for school. "His father and I are very proud. It will be interesting to see how it all turns out. He's living a very exciting life these days."

"I think it's going to do a lot of good!"

"Well, we should get going," I said to Mom.

"I told Benji to take as many days as he needs for this project. Just keep us posted," said Mrs. Petty.

"I will," I promised. Mom and I walked out of the office. She didn't say a word until we got in the car and closed the doors.

"What was that all about?" she asked. "Your father said you guys signed a paper saying you wouldn't talk about the dinosaurs to anyone."

"Who said I mentioned anything about the dinosaurs to the principal?" I asked.

"You didn't make up some crazy excuse to get out of school did you?" questioned Mom.

"Nope, I told her the truth," I said.

"The whole truth?"

I cracked a small smile. "I just left out the parts about the dinosaurs."

I may also have mentioned something about making a sizeable donation to the school. How does the Benjamin "Benji" Franklin Mega Media Center sound?

CHAPTER 9

A Dino-Mite Plan!

Word spread quickly that I was working on a project at the old airport. The fact that trucks containing cows, chickens, and huge sheets of thick plastic were rolling through town may have helped. Our town is pretty small. Anytime something out of the ordinary happens, people know.

That afternoon, I met with Dr. Snow and Dr. Kent in a small office located near the hangar. Workers were assembling the high-security plastic into three large containers.

"When this thing's over, people will wonder what was going on back here," I said. "We'll have to work fast and get this done the first time. If everything goes as planned, I'll have the Troodon safely captured and loaded on a truck. You'll have to relocate them somewhere far from here."

"I already have a place lined up," Dr. Snow said. "It's perfectly safe, secure, and secluded."

"Fantastic!" I exclaimed. "By tomorrow morning, the town won't know any of this ever happened. Dr. Snow, if all goes as planned, I have one more thing I'm going to need from you guys."

"Anything, Benji," Dr. Snow agreed. "If you get us out of this dinosaur mess, you just say the word."

"I'll need you guys to give me the old airport," I told him. "In return, I'll donate funds to help you guys keep the Troodon out of trouble."

"No need for that, Benji," Dr. Kent said. "If you manage to save the day and recapture the Troodon safely, you'll have earned this airport." She reached out and shook my hand.

"What do you want the airport for?" Dr. Snow asked. "A personal jet?"

"No, I don't plan to do any flying," I said. (Besides, my own private jet was in the repair shop.)

"It'll be a gruesome scene if the Troodon attack the cows and chickens," Dr. Kent said, changing the subject.

"Don't worry about it," I said.

"What about all those cows and chickens?" Dr. Snow asked. "I think you may have gone a bit overboard on the bait. We've managed to lure the Troodon in with only a few steaks."

"You also haven't managed to catch them yet," I pointed out. "Just trust me."

$ $ $

The team and I worked all day setting up my plan. We built three large enclosures out of the thick, clear plastic. In one, we built a corral for the cows and in another a huge coop for the chickens. They were completely enclosed with the exception of airholes in the top. Nothing could get in or out.

The enclosures were placed right next to each other in the far field behind the old hangar.

The plastic was so clear that from a distance you couldn't see it at all.

In front of those enclosures, we placed the third. The third was identical to the other two, except the side facing the woods, where we knew the Troodon were hiding, was designed to be remotely lowered once they entered the structure.

The first part of my plan was that the Troodon would see and smell the cows and chickens. Once it was dark, they would come out of the woods to prey on the farm animals. They would mistakenly enter the empty container thinking they could reach the cows and chickens. But, when they were inside, I'd remotely close the fourth wall and capture them.

The plan was simple enough. If it worked, everyone would be amazed. I just had to pull it off without anything going wrong.

By the time night fell, everything was in place. There was only one thing left to do...

Find the Troodon.

The remote-control helicopter that I ordered had a night-vision camera mounted on the front. I flew it over the woods where we knew the Troodon were hiding.

"Do you think this will work?" Dad asked.

"I'm not sure," I said, concentrating on the remote. "But there's only one way to find out."

I flew the helicopter behind the Troodon. I didn't want them going in the opposite direction of the enclosure. They caught the scent of the cows and chickens because they were moving toward them. I followed close behind.

When the Troodon reached the edge of the woods, the dinos all stopped. I hovered above with the helicopter. The creatures seemed to be analyzing the situation. It was like a full buffet just waiting for them, but they were super cautious.

Over the course of an hour, the dinosaurs inched closer and closer toward the glass enclosure.

I was so afraid they would see their reflections and get spooked, but luckily that didn't happen. A cloudy sky hid the moonlight.

One after the other, the Troodon went inside. They walked to the far side of the enclosure thinking they'd be able to reach the cows and chickens.

Once they were all safely inside, I clicked the button and closed the enclosure with the fourth wall. *Yes!* I let out a sigh of relief, and Dr. Snow and his team cheered. For the first time since I'd met him, Dr. Clive smiled.

It worked like a charm. The Troodon were safely captured. We loaded the enclosure holding the dinosaurs onto a flat bed truck. Dr. Snow's team covered the beds with old semi trailers taken from grandpa's workshop.

Within a few hours, a truck bearing the logo "Ocean Wave Underwear" rolled out the front gate of the airport. The Troodon were on their way to a safe new location.

CHAPTER 10

Food for Thought

In the morning, I called Mom and told her to come out to the old airport. An hour later, I met her at the entrance.

Everyone else had gone with Dr. Snow to set up the Troodon in their new location. Dad and I had spent the night at the old airport and completed the second phase of my plan with the carpenters.

"How did it go last night?" Mom asked.

"You would have been very proud," Dad said. "Your son was like a hero without the cape and the silly suit."

"I can't say I'm surprised," she said. "He's always been brilliant."

"Thanks, Mom," I said. "But I have a surprise for you, too."

"You bought the dinosaurs as pets?" she asked.

"Haha. Funny, Mom," I said.

Dad and I climbed in her car and drove around to the back of the property, where the cows and chickens were located.

Overnight, Dad and I had released them into the field. It was completely fenced in, and they were free to roam. The main hangar was a perfect barn. The chickens were set up in the other hangar, which we turned into a giant chicken coop.

"I didn't know this was a farm. I thought it was all just abandoned," Mom said.

"It was, sort of. The cows and chickens are new. So are the two greenhouses," I said. The clear plastic enclosures made perfect greenhouses for growing crops.

"I don't get it," Mom said, puzzled. "What was the project you and your dad were working on up here? Where are the dinosaurs you told me about?"

"They're gone. Dr. Snow and his team are taking them somewhere safe," I explained. "In return for my help, I convinced them to give me all this land. I thought a farm might help solve the food shortage at the pantry. I think with all these cows and chickens your pantry will be sustainable now."

"What are you talking about, Benji?" Mom asked.

"Remember when you told me to let you know when I'd found a better way?" I asked. "I'm saying this farm is yours."

Mom opened her mouth to say something, but nothing came out. Instead, she gave me a hug.

"And I put several million dollars in an account," I said. "You can hire farmers to work the land and take care of the animals. You can buy trucks and staff to deliver the food. Whatever you need, I've got you covered."

"I don't know what to say," Mom exclaimed. "I'm amazed at what goes on in that brain of yours, Benjamin."

I thought about telling her that Troodon could be trained to make excellent pets. But I figured that could wait until after breakfast!

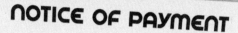

BADR INSTITUTE

NOTICE OF PAYMENT

FROM:
B.A.D.R. Institute

TO:
Benjamin "Benji" Franklin

PAYMENT DUE UPON RECEIPT

ITEM:	QUANTITY:	AMOUNT:
Remote helicopter with HD night-vision video camera	1	$12,341
High-security glass	15,000 ft.	$1,765,000
Dairy Cows	114	$25,792
Chickens	225	$1,287.64
Cash		$6,000,000

TOTAL COST: $7,804,420.64

Moo!

PAID!

CHAPTER 11

Asteroids!

The next morning, I was out in the workshop downloading data from the satellite. Dad was back working on his magnetic suits. He'd reversed the magnets and his safety system seemed about ready for a real-life trial. He had a fisherman in town that agreed to try it out with his crew. He'd dropped his boat off at our workshop earlier in the morning, and Dad was installing the system in the boat.

That's when I saw it...

An asteroid appeared on the satellite's data system. It was on course to collide with Earth!

"You might want to take a look at this, Dad," I said, my heart pounding.

He was by the boat, twisting at something with his wrench. "I can't right now, Benji. Is it good news or bad?" he asked.

"Both," I said.

"Well, does it look like something's going to take out our satellite?" he asked.

"Well, no, and that's part of the good news," I told him. "The bad news...it might take out the planet. The WHOLE planet!!"

My dad is super organized. Everything he owns has a place, and he always puts things where they belong. I thought it was kind of funny that even though there was an asteroid screaming toward the planet, the first thing he did was put his wrench carefully back in his toolbox. If there was a time to simply drop it on the floor and be sloppy, this was it!

"What's the other good news?" asked Dad.

"Maybe we can stop it," I said.

"Benji, this asteroid is rushing toward Earth at incredible speed. I don't think we can do anything," he said, skeptical.

"From my calculations, the asteroid is still sixty days from impact," I explained.

"Then I wouldn't panic just yet," he said. "I've seen space debris that looked like it was on course for impact suddenly change direction and sail right on by. Now, it's getting late. You need to get to the bus stop."

Huh?!? How can he expect me to go to school after what I just told him? "I don't think you heard me when I screamed, 'the WHOLE planet,'" I said. "I need to track this asteroid and send the data to someone who can help save us! Then maybe I can buy a laser canon...or a supersized missile launcher...or a titanium flyswatter the size of a football field, or—"

"Benji, you're in sixth grade," he said. "The world can survive without you on this one. You're not the only person with a satellite tracking this thing. Everything will be fine."

Obviously, I didn't agree, but I could tell there was no way Dad was going to let me stay home.

$ $ $

On the ride to school, all I could think about was the asteroid. I was working on my smartphone, which was really hard to do with the bus bouncing and all the kids talking. I made a list of the ways to destroy or send an asteroid off course:

HOW TO STOP THE ASTEROID

1. Blow to bits.

2. Send off course with mega-ton explosion.

3. Redirect course with giant sail.

4. Jackhammer to pieces with high-tech machines.

5. Create a chemical reaction to disintegrate.

I was so focused on my list that I didn't notice this person sitting next to me. Cindy Meyers. "You know, you're not allowed to use your smartphone on the bus," she said. "You think just because your app is so popular that you can do whatever you want?"

I rolled my eyes. "Good morning to you, too, Cindy," I said, trying to be polite. "I'm busy on an important project. It's not like I'm playing video games or texting like you."

"I'm not texting or talking on my phone because that would be against school rules," she whined.

"I'll be watching," I said, getting back to work.

"That makes two of us," she warned. "It's going to be a real shame when the principal takes your smartphone away and bans you from the bus."

"If you knew what I was working on you wouldn't be giving me a hard time," I said.

She laughed. "I find that hard to believe."

Cindy had always been difficult, but she was being extra annoying today.

"What's your problem?" I asked.

"I don't have a problem," she said. "You're the one who thinks you're so cool ever since you created that ridiculous computer app."

"Who said I think I'm cool?" I said. "For your information, I've never been considered cool."

"Well, you don't act like it. You created that app, and then you didn't even have to come to school because you're a big shot now. You weren't the only one who worked hard on that app project," she said.

She was upset that her app didn't get more attention than mine. I couldn't even remember what her app did! "I haven't been to school because I was busy helping out the food shelter," I explained.

"I think you're a troublemaker," she said.

"Then why'd you sit next to me?" I asked. I had bigger things to think about than Cindy.

"Because I'm on the School Decency Committee and you're on my radar," Cindy explained. "You haven't been around to see the damage your app created. Kids are making up all kinds of excuses for things thanks to your reckless idea."

I got a little anxious because I had barely been to school since I created the app. I knew tons of people had downloaded it, but I hadn't had any time to see how kids were using it.

"Well," I began, "I'm about to see for myself."

CHAPTER 12
Big Trouble

Everything seemed pretty much the same as usual when I got to school. My app wasn't causing any problems as far as I could see. I was definitely getting more attention than usual though. More people seemed to know my name, which was funny because before the app I wasn't exactly popular.

On my way to tech class, a few kids patted me on the back. I didn't like all the attention. It was a little stressful. I found myself walking quicker than usual. I slipped into my seat in tech class, relieved to be out of the hall.

Mrs. Heart started the lesson by welcoming me back to school. The class erupted with applause. "You're a superstar these days," she said. "We've been following your success online. I can't believe how huge your app, Excuse Yourself, has become."

I'd been so busy with the Troodon and Dr. Snow that I hadn't had time to read what was being said about the app.

"I'm pretty shocked myself," I said. "Honestly, I haven't been able to follow what's going on with the app because I've been working."

"I thought you were out because of the app," Mrs. Heart said curiously.

"Actually, I was busy with another project for the food pantry," I explained. "The principal, Mrs. Petty, gave me permission to take a few days to work on it. Remember?"

"That's not an excuse, is it?" Mrs. Heart joked.

"No, but maybe I should add it to the app," I said with a smile.

"Are you rich?" said a student in the back.

"It's not polite to ask someone a question like that," said Mrs. Heart. "We're all very happy for you though, Benji."

Realizing that everyone at school knew I made a TON of money was kind of embarrassing. James, the kid sitting next to me, leaned over and whispered, "How much do you actually have?"

"I don't know," I said, which was basically the truth because the number was always changing. I'd checked the total before school, but there were too many zeros to count!

CHA-CHING! CHA-CHING!!

I'd only been out of school for a week, but it felt like a year.

$ $ $

When I got home later that day, I went straight to the workshop. Dad was at the computer and looked like he'd been there all day.

"Benji, I was wrong," he said. "People don't seem to be tracking this thing. You've found something that others haven't noticed yet. I can see why! It's not a known asteroid. I've been searching the database all day and can't find any record of it."

"What does that mean?" I asked.

"We might be the only ones who know it's there," he exclaimed. "Most satellites are designed to locate asteroids larger than a kilometer. My satellite is great at detecting asteroids *smaller* than a kilometer. This one is about the size of a twenty-story building, so it's much harder to locate than a larger one."

I did the math in my head. A story on a building is about twelve feet high. If the asteroid was twenty stories, it measured about 240 feet long!

"That's small?" I asked.

"Compared to some larger asteroids," said Dad. "It's big enough to cause a lot of damage, but still small enough to go undetected. The good news is it won't destroy the planet, but if it hits it will do some real damage."

"Shouldn't we call someone or notify the government?" I asked.

"Not yet," he said. "Let's give it a few days and see if it changes course. We have some time."

I logged on to my computer to research the kind of damage an asteroid would do if it impacted Earth. I learned that the asteroid that caused the extinction of the dinosaurs was about six miles wide.

The asteroid I located wasn't even close to the size of that one, but it was large enough to level buildings for five miles from the impact location.

I worked to try and calculate the impact date. I knew Dad was doing the same.

ASTEROIDS

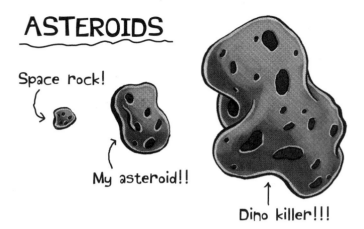

Space rock!

My asteroid!!

Dino killer!!!

Neither one of us said anything for about an hour. Then, I broke the silence.

"If my calculations are correct," I said. "The asteroid will hit Earth on Mom's birthday!"

I didn't have the heart to tell Mom that the world could be blasted by an asteroid on her birthday. When I went out to the farm later that night, I didn't say anything about it.

Mom hadn't wasted any time taking over the farm I'd bought her. It was already producing milk and eggs, and she had a full-time staff. She also bought a few refrigerated trucks for deliveries. That night, she was checking on the chickens, as I walked alongside her.

"You've been on your computer too long again," she said. "Your eyes are all bloodshot."

"No more than usual," I said.

She stopped and took another look at me. "What's on your mind, Benji? You look troubled."

"I'm fine, Mom. Today was my first day back to school. It was a little strange. Kids are really focused on the app and all the money I'm making." I said this knowing it was partially true, and my real concern was the asteroid.

"Kids your age don't normally experience this kind of success," she said. "It's natural for your friends to be confused and ask a lot of questions."

"I guess," I replied.

"There's something else that you're not telling me," she said. "What is it?"

I couldn't lie to my mother. "Our satellite located an asteroid this morning. It's on track to smash Earth in about a month."

"I know. Your father told me a few hours ago," she said, walking ahead of me.

"WHAT?! Why didn't you tell me that?"

"I wanted to see if you'd tell me on your own. Why didn't you tell me?" she said.

"I didn't want to worry you," I explained.

"I'm not worried, Benji."

"You should be!" I exclaimed. "It's on a collision course with the planet. The WHOLE planet!"

"You'll figure something out," she suggested.

Mothers. They're always so supportive. But this problem was a little out of my league.

"I bet you already have a solution brewing inside that head, and you don't even know it yet," she said. "You don't want an asteroid ruining your mother's birthday, do you?"

CHAPTER 13
Spacing Out

I went for a walk by myself on the trails behind the farm. I couldn't help feeling that a Troodon was going to jump out at me from behind a tree.

It was pretty surreal when I stopped to think about how much things had changed in such a short time. It was hard to even remember a time before Excuse Yourself.

As I walked, I imagined scenarios that might change the course of the asteroid or destroy it. I'd read online once that if you blow up the asteroid it becomes a bunch of small asteroids instead of one big one. The group of smaller ones acts like a shotgun blast and can cause even more damage!

My mind kept cycling through all the scenarios I'd listed on my computer. There simply had to be a solution.

Instead of blowing up the asteroid, what if there was a way to capture it? I wondered. I could land some sort of remote-control unit on it and simply fly it like a spaceship.

I tripped on a large stone and stopped to pick it up. I held it in my hands for a while wondering how I could stop it if it were hurtling through space at thousands of miles per hour.

I threw it as hard as I could and watched it sail into the woods. I picked up another stone and hurled it the same direction. A vision of a net wrapping around the stone came to me.

A net would stop or slow the stone down, but I couldn't figure out how to get a large net into space. Even if I did, could I could change the course of an asteroid?

I picked up another stone, and my phone rang.

"Hey, Dad," I answered.

"Hi, Benji," he said. "I just spoke with Dr. Snow. He has someone he'd like you to meet."

"The Troodon didn't escape again, did they?" I asked, hoping that wasn't the case.

"Nope, the dinos are safe and sound," Dad said. "This is about the asteroid. Why don't you have Mom drive you home? We need to talk."

$ $ $

When I got home, Dad was sifting through old airplane parts in the back field. "What's up?" I asked.

He climbed out from the rusted cockpit of a small plane and sat on the wing. "Come on over," he said, dusting off a place for me to sit.

"What are you doing?" I asked.

"I'm looking for spare parts to see if I can make another low-orbit rocket," he said, "but I wanted you to come home to talk about Dr. Snow."

"What did he say?" I asked.

"He asked my permission to give our number to another scientist," he explained.

"Why?" I asked.

"He said he wasn't sure, but that a very prominent scientist contacted him for help, and he suggested you."

"What did you say?"

"That between the Troodon and Excuse Yourself you've been busy," said Dad. "It might be good to take a little break."

"I'm fine, Dad," I assured him. "I'm too rich to take a break."

Just then, my phone rang.

"Hello," I said.

From the other side, in an English accent, a man's voice said, "Hello, Benjamin. My name is Sir Robert Dransling. You come highly recommended by Dr. Snow."

"That was fast," I said.

"There's no time to waste," he replied. "A situation has come to my attention in the past twenty-four hours that causes me great concern. If my information is correct, you've noticed this—ahem—problem as well."

"You mean the asteroid?" I asked.

"SHHHHH!" he said. "Someone might hear you. If people learn there's an asteroid on a collision course with the planet, they will go completely loopy. Discretion is the best course, lad. We mustn't breathe a word of this to anyone else."

I looked around at the back field, the rusty plane, and Dad. "My lips are sealed," I said.

"I'll send for you tomorrow," he said. "I'm flying you out to New Mexico so we can talk in person."

"But I have school tomorrow—"

"I'll see you tomorrow, Mr. Franklin. There's not a moment to waste." Then he hung up.

"He wants me in New Mexico tomorrow," I said.

"You have school," said Dad, "and I'm doing my first test of the magnetic system out at sea."

"We'll figure something out," I told Dad.

"Who was that man anyway?" he asked.

"He said his name was Sir Robert Dransling," I replied.

"Sir Robert Dransling?!" Dad exclaimed. "He's a world leader in space technology. They say he'll be the first person to provide space flights to tourists as a vacation!"

Really? I thought. *Maybe he can help me with my space station zoo idea!*

CHAPTER 14

Riding in Style

I went to school the next day like any other day. The phone rang in my math class. My teacher answered and then told me to head down to the office because I was going home early.

The secretary at the front desk and Mrs. Petty, the principal, looked confused.

"Benji, your father called and told us to release you early," Mrs. Petty said.

I looked around the room. "Who's picking me up?" I asked.

The secretary pointed outside. Through the window, I could see a long black limousine parked in front of the school. Its windows were tinted, and there was a tiny British flag painted on the passenger door.

"What's that?" I asked.

"We were hoping you could tell us," said the principal. "It's highly unusual for a student to be picked up by a non-family member."

"Who's in the limo?" I asked.

"Your father wouldn't say," she told me. "He just said that he was out at sea and your mother was out of town on business for the pantry and that a limo would be by to pick you up."

"All right then," I said. "I'm free to go?"

"Yes, I hope everything is fine," Mrs. Petty said.

When she said, "I hope everything is fine," I realized that she thought something was wrong. Based on her expression, she probably thought someone in my family had died or something.

"Everything is fine," I said.

"Keep up that positive attitude," Mrs. Petty said.

When I walked out, a man stepped out of the driver's seat and opened the back door. I realized that all the classes facing the front of the building were full of kids pressed up against the windows.

"Good morning, Mr. Franklin," the chauffeur said in a British accent.

"Nice car," I said. I wasn't sure what else to say to him. My heart was racing pretty fast.

"I realize this is highly unusual," he said. "However, we are in the midst of a decidedly unusual circumstance. Your father is returning from the fishing vessel he's on, and he asked us to pick you up in order to save time. I have your mother on a live video chat."

He held out his phone, and I could see Mom on the screen. "Hi, Benji," she said. "I'm already on the road and your father is on the boat. Sir Robert sent this car for you. It's going to take you to meet Dad at the dock, and then you're off."

"Off to where?" I asked.

"Your father has all the details," she said. "I wish I could tag along, but I'm halfway to Shiny Desert to make my delivery."

"Okay, Mom," I said. "Does this mean I'll be out of school for a few days?"

"I don't know, honey," she said.

The chauffeur nodded his head to indicate that I would in fact be out for a few days. I gave him a thumbs-up.

"You've already missed too many days," said Mom. "I don't want you missing too much more. But, this seems like the opportunity of a lifetime, and I'll let your father decide. He'll be with you the whole time. Have fun, and give me a call later to let me know how things are going."

$$\$ \, \$ \, \$$

During the ride to pick up Dad, the driver kept the glass wall between the front seat and the back of the limo shut. It was a little strange sitting alone in the back of that huge car. I ate a few bags of peanuts and watched some television.

I may have to buy one of these, I thought. *And maybe one for Mom, too. Then she wouldn't have to drive herself to places like Shiny Desert all alone.*

Dad hopped in when we reached the docks. He was wearing one of his magnetic fisherman suits.

"How is the suit working?" I asked.

"Really well," he said. "But we've only tested it in calm water. I'll have to increase the magnetic force on the boat for it to work correctly in rough seas."

I was wondering how long it was going to take Dad to acknowledge that I was out of school on a weekday. And that we were being driven in a limo by a complete stranger.

"Sounds great," I said. "Anything else going on?"

"Not really," he replied.

I watched him checking out the TV for a while until he finally snapped out it. "What's the deal? Where are we going?" he asked.

"Are you going to wear that magnetic suit the whole time?" I said.

Dad quickly unscrewed his helmet. "Where are we going, Benji?"

"I thought you knew," I said.

The glass partition between the front and back seat suddenly slid down. The chauffeur glanced toward us over his shoulder. "We're driving to the airport," he said.

"But where are we going?" I said.

"The desert," he told us.

"Desert?" cried Dad. "Which one? Besides, I'm not dressed for the desert!"

The glass wall smoothly slid upward and cut us off again from the driver.

"How many deserts are in New Mexico?" I asked.

The rest of the ride Dad told me all about Sir Robert Dransling. He sounded like a wildly successful guy. He owned newspapers, shipping businesses, TV stations, radio stations, and a ton of technology companies. He'd even been knighted by the Queen of England!

Why did he need me?

CHAPTER 15

Up, Up, and Away

We drove up to a special gate at the airport. Security guards opened it, and we drove right onto the runway. It was a special section of the airport for all the private jets.

"Wow!" Dad said. He's been a plane nut ever since he was a kid.

I lowered the divider between the driver and us. "Are we going on one of these jets?" I asked.

"The one at the end," he said.

At the end of all the amazing jets was the coolest one of all. It looked like a bullet with wings.

"That's the ECS Bolt 41," Dad said.

"I see you know your aircraft," the driver said. "But that's actually the ECS Bolt 42. It's *next* year's model. No one else has anything like it."

"It looks like half plane, half space ship," I said.

"You could say that. Ah, we are here," he said, stopping the car. He climbed out and politely opened my door.

Dad and I stepped out.

A long staircase slowly lowered from the plane. A man stood at the top. He waved.

"That's Sir Robert Dransling," whispered Dad.

Sir Robert was super tan, like he'd been in the sun every day of his life. I was surprised he wasn't in a business suit or at least dressed up a little. He wore flip-flops and one of those brightly colored Hawaiian shirts.

He shook my hand. "Mr. Franklin, please climb aboard and make yourself at home," he said.

I'd been on a plane two other times in my life: once to Florida and once to California. On both of those trips, we flew on a regular plane.

This plane was straight out of a movie.

The luxury aircraft looked like an expensive hotel. There were actual rooms. It had a living room, kitchen, and even a few bedrooms.

"Can I get you gentlemen something to eat?" asked Sir Robert.

"We'd love a few turkey sandwiches, if it's not too much trouble," Dad said. "I've been out on the water all morning, and Benjamin didn't have a chance to eat lunch yet."

Sir Robert pressed a button on his phone. "Done," he said. "They will be out in a few minutes."

"That's pretty cool," I said.

"I agree," he said. "It's very cool. From what I hear about you, young Benjamin, you could buy a plane like this of your own."

"Maybe I will," I said.

"I didn't make my first million until I was twenty-five," said Sir Robert. "From what I understand, you're only twelve, and you're way beyond that."

"Benjamin hasn't had a whole lot of time to really think about the money he's made," my dad explained. "He's been busy working for Dr. Snow since the app was released."

"I've also been helping my mother establish a small farm for the food pantry she runs," I added.

"Intelligent, modest, and giving. You might just be my new favorite person, young Benji," Sir Robert said.

Just then, a waiter handed me a plate with a turkey sandwich and a soda.

"And you might be mine," I said, smiling and raising my glass.

"I can offer you much more than a simple sandwich, Benji," said Sir Robert. "I contacted you because I know that you have a low-orbit satellite collecting data on space debris. I have several of my own in orbit. My team and I first spotted the asteroid a few days ago. I realized that you and I were probably the only two people with satellites designed to identify an asteroid of that size."

"It was very cool of you to invite us here," I said. "But what exactly can we do for you?"

"It's what I think we may be able to accomplish together," he replied. "My focus in life is on helping others reach their full potential. I'm sure my team could figure out some way to deflect or destroy this asteroid, but I'm more interested in what *you* would do with it, Benji."

"Since you're so wealthy, don't you have access to the world's best scientists?" I asked. "Why are you asking me?"

"Indeed I do have access to the world's best and brightest," he said. "However, as I've already pointed out, you seem to be the only other person to spot the asteroid. If the 'world's best scientists' haven't even been able to locate the asteroid, why would I want their help in trying to destroy it?"

I thought about what he said for a moment. It was kind of amazing that no one else had detected an asteroid that could possibly level cities and towns if nothing was done to change its course.

"The reason I asked you here is that I believe you're an extraordinary young man," Sir Robert continued. "I told Dr. Snow that having those Troodon was going to become a problem. What surprised me was when he told me a twelve-year-old solved the problem for him. I'd like to know what you'd do to solve this asteroid situation."

"I have an idea," I said. "I wouldn't blow it up, I'd try to land it."

"I'm listening," he said.

"It'll be expensive," I said.

"Too expensive for a couple of zillionaires like us?" he said, smiling.

"Never," I said. "Have you ever heard of graphene?"

CHAPTER 16
The Asteroid Net

Of course Sir Robert had heard of graphene. It's only the most exciting new material on the planet. It's super thin and light, but graphene is also the strongest material known to man.

A few years ago, two scientists won the Nobel Prize for their work with graphene. They said it's so strong that a piece of graphene as thin as plastic wrap is strong enough to hold an elephant!

"We've worked a little with graphene at my facility. An incredible material," Sir Robert said.

"Is it as amazing as people say?" I asked.

"It's flexible, incredibly strong, and can conduct electricity," he said. "It's a miracle material."

Dad and I knew all about graphene. We'd read articles and watched a lot of videos on it. Still, we'd never actually seen it in person.

"Do you have graphene at your facility now?" Dad asked.

"We do," Sir Robert replied. "We plan to use it a great deal in the future, in everything from cell phones to airplanes. But the technology isn't very advanced yet."

"Do you think a giant sheet of it would be strong enough to catch an asteroid?" I asked.

"It's definitely strong enough to catch the asteroid without breaking," he said. "But it would be almost impossible to predict where the asteroid will impact earth. The odds of placing the graphene mesh in the right place is a million-to-one shot."

"I'm not talking about catching the asteroid on Earth," I explained. "I'm talking about catching it in space before it enters the atmosphere. You could use one of your spaceships to get the mesh up there."

Sir Robert stood up and walked over to a large thin computer screen on the wall. He clicked the controls a few times and opened what looked like an animation program. "Benji, come over here," he said. "Let's see if we can't get a sense of exactly what you're talking about."

Dad and I walked over to the screen.

"Tell it what you're thinking," said Sir Robert. "The program will create a visual model."

"You're kidding!" I exclaimed.

"You're not the only person capable of creating a cool computer program, Benji," he said. "If you describe your idea to this program, it will show us what the concept will look like. Give it a go."

"Okay." I had the idea formed in my head, but it was tricky explaining it to the computer program clearly enough so it could create a visual model for us. "We launch a rocket into space containing a graphene mesh long enough and wide enough to catch the asteroid," I began.

The screen immediately displayed an animation of a rocket deploying a long thin sheet in space.

I continued. "Four other rockets would then attach themselves to each corner of the sheet. These rockets would be able to hover in space, holding each corner of the sheet in place to capture the asteroid as it zooms toward Earth."

The high-tech machine took a few seconds, but the screen created an animation similar to the images I had imagined.

"This program is absolutely amazing!" I said.

"Much cooler than a turkey sandwich?" Sir Robert joked.

"Let's hear the rest of your idea, Benji," Dad said. "Don't lose your concentration."

"Well, when the asteroid makes contact with the mesh, the four rockets will fire," I said. "This would allow us to remotely lower the asteroid to Earth safely."

I couldn't believe that in only a few minutes the program managed to create what I was seeing in my mind. I had worried that the plan was a little far-fetched, but seeing it there on the screen, I felt it was possible.

"Begin production of materials," Sir Robert told the program.

"What will that do?" I asked.

"It will send the plans to my team, and they can get to work on it right away."

"That's astonishing," Dad said.

"It's technology, Mr. Franklin."

"I love it," I said.

"You haven't seen anything yet," Sir Robert said.

$ $ $

We touched down about three hours later at his facility in the desert. The place looked like a scene from *Star Wars*. There were several buildings built around what looked like a futuristic airport.

People worked busily everywhere I looked.

He had more jets, race cars, and rockets than I could have imagined. Many of them looked like rockets that had been used a long time ago. "I'm a bit of a collector," he said.

The luxury aircraft came to a stop, and we climbed out and onto the runway. He and Dad talked about the early days of aviation as he gave us a tour of his facility. I could tell Dad was having the time of his life. As the sun was setting Sir Robert said, "I'd like to show you gentlemen my most prized project. Follow me."

We walked to a large building on the far side of the runway. It was buzzing with activity. There were people in bright red suits assembling what looked like spacecraft.

"This is the future, Benji," said Sir Robert. "You're looking at my prize possession. It's the next step in aviation and the craft that will lead humanity into space in large numbers."

I couldn't believe what I was seeing. It was the most advanced rocket ship I'd ever seen, and I'd seen them all online before.

"This is a top secret machine," he continued. "Every part you see is made right here at the space center. I don't take any chances on getting a poor product or on other people learning what I'm up to. I hope I can count on you two to help keep my secret."

"Of course," Dad said.

"I'm just trying to figure out what it can do," I said, looking at the scene in front of me. This wasn't a sci-fi movie. This was the real deal!

"These are low-orbit ships," explained Sir Robert. "Their missions will be programmed ahead of time and no pilots are needed. All you do is open the door, get in, and off you go into the great beyond. Space tourists will get into low orbit, take a few pictures, shoot some video, and basically have the time of their lives."

"It's the coolest idea I've ever heard!" I said.

"We have several ships completed and ready to go. I was just waiting for the right time to test them. We'll use your asteroid plan as the reason to launch them into space."

CHAPTER 17

Suit Up!

That night, Mom called to see how things were going and check if I'd be going to school the next day. Dad told her that the things I was experiencing were too extraordinary to miss and I would probably be out for a few days.

After dinner, one of Sir Robert's assistants showed Dad and me to a small building at the edge of the airport. "You gentlemen will be staying here for the next few days, so make yourselves comfortable," he said. "Please let me know if you need anything."

He gave us each a laptop that accessed my data from Dad's satellite and gave us access to all of Sir Robert's data, too. His satellites were so much more advanced than the one Dad launched. They even had live video feeds from space.

Dad and I were up half the night checking out the satellite data. We must have fallen asleep really late because the next thing I knew, it was morning. I was drooling on the couch and Dad was snoring on the floor.

There was a knock at the front door. It was Sir Robert. He came in and sat next to me on the couch. "I see that you two are settling in."

"We spent most of the night exploring your satellites," Dad said. "They're really fantastic!"

"That's kind of you to say, but I'm just as amazed that you got something up into orbit that functions as a satellite using scrap parts," he said to Dad.

"You haven't seen our property," I said. "It's not your average scrap heap. It's like a storage yard full of everything you can imagine. Dad's been messing around with mechanical things for so long he can build anything."

"I'm just a hobby builder," Dad said.

"My own father was the same way," Dad added. "One time he built me a hovercraft out of a wading pool, a microwave oven, and an electric toothbrush."

"That's absolutely amazing!" Sir Robert said.

"Yeah," said Dad. "It didn't go very far, but I had the cleanest teeth in the state."

"I grew up in private schools full of nannies and tutors," Sir Robert said. "I've always been book smart, but I've never been a do-it-yourself-er. It's good for me to spend this time with you two. You're true inventors in the purest sense."

"And *you're* a super inventor," I told him. "This place is like Disneyland."

"I'm happy to share it with you," he replied, smiling. "We have a busy day planned, but I thought we could have a little fun before we rolled up our sleeves and got to work today."

"Can we fly in one of your ships?" I asked.

"There's no better time than the present."

The ship he showed us could carry two to four passengers. Sir Robert pressed a button on the outside of the ship and three seats popped up. They were large, comfortable-looking and sat next to each other in an arc.

The ship was like a large toy. It reminded me of a WaveRunner, but about three times the size. It had small wings on each side. It looked like it could be part of a ride at an amusement park. I couldn't believe this little thing would be able to carry us into outer space.

"Can it really take us into outer orbit?" I asked.

"It's more than capable. In fact, I think you'll be surprised at how easily the Day Tripper can take us on a round-trip. Are you gents ready for your first taste of space?"

Dad looked like he was about to pop with excitement. If he were a kid he'd be jumping up and down. "I'm ready," Dad said. "I've been ready for this moment since I was a kid."

"Me too," I said sarcastically.

"Benji, when your father and I were children people thought that we'd be able to visit space in our lifetime. But technology didn't deliver it fast enough for me. That's why I decided to create the technology I wanted on my own terms."

"Have you been up before?" I asked.

"This will be my tenth trip up. Only a handful of people have been up so far. I'm proud to inform you that you'll be the first, uh, non-adult I put into space."

A man rolled up to us with a cart containing three folded-up space suits. "Here are the suits you requested, Sir Robert."

"Thank you, Arthur. We'll be off in about ten minutes. Please alert the team and the tower."

"Will do, sir."

Before I knew it, Dad was seated on the floor and had his suit half on. "Well, I'm thrilled to see you're so excited," Mr. Dransling said. "Let's suit up and get up there!"

Moments later, we were seated in the ship. It really did feel like an amusement park ride. When the engine turned on, it wasn't as loud as I'd expected.

I sat in the middle seat between Dad and Sir Robert. The control panel was really simple. I'd expected it to be full of gadgets and gizmos, but it wasn't. There were cameras showing us a view of the rear and each side of the craft. There was a touch screen in front of each seat giving data such as time, temperature, speed, and so on.

There were several interactive touch tabs: tower comm, video, e-mail, notes, music, and GPS.

That was it. The inside of the ship was simple, clean, and really modern. There was even a drink holder. I wondered if it really kept the drinks in the holder or they simply flew around the ship once it reached zero gravity.

Ah, zero G!! I'd always wanted to go to space, and I'm sure the view is amazing, but the real reason I'd always wanted to go to space was to experience weightlessness.

"Sir Robert, will we be able to experience zero gravity in the ship?" I asked.

"Of course!" he said. "What would a trip to outer space be without experiencing zero G?"

"But, the cockpit ceiling is so low and the area we're sitting in is so tight," Dad said. "I don't understand."

"Trust me. You'll experience zero gravity."

We all buckled in and the ship pulled slowly out of the hangar.

It was a perfect day; there wasn't a cloud in the sky. We rolled along the runway, picking up speed. In twenty seconds, the front tipped up and the ship took flight. It was amazing how safe I felt.

We slowly gained altitude. Before I knew it, we were above the clouds. "How are you guys feeling?" Sir Robert asked.

"Fantastic," I said. "I can't believe we don't need helmets or anything."

"I'm so used to seeing astronauts in heavy gear," Dad added.

"That was one of my main goals with this little ship," said Sir Robert. "I wanted the passengers to feel like they were in a car."

"Or an X-wing fighter!" I said.

"Go ahead and recline if you'd like. The button is on the side of your seat. When we get into outer orbit you may want to lay your seat back completely to get a better look at the stars."

"I'm fine," I said feeling my first bit of nervousness. I didn't want to admit that I was worried, but all of a sudden I was getting more and more nervous by the minute.

The numbers showing our altitude were climbing so fast I couldn't read them and the speed was picking up pretty dramatically. We were climbing quickly. I knew that in a matter of minutes we'd either be in outer space or in a million pieces!

I thought about Mom and how she'd be worried out of her mind if she knew what Dad and I were doing. "Can I call my mom once we're out of Earth's orbit?" I asked.

"Of course. You can call her whenever you like," Sir Robert said. I relaxed a little and couldn't wait to get high enough to see Earth as a blue ball floating in space.

The ship climbed and climbed until I could feel a difference. The engine cut off and the ship seemed to float.

"Did you know that once you've reached an altitude of 50 miles above the planet you are, by definition, an astronaut?" Sir Robert asked.

I looked at the touch screen and we were at 62 miles and counting.

"Welcome to space, gentlemen," he said.

It was such a strange sensation looking back on the planet. It was just like I'd seen it in videos and pictures, but it was real.

Dad literally had a tear in his eye.

For a split second, I felt like I might cry (or throw up!). It was overwhelming.

I was in outer space!

CHAPTER 18

Zero Gravity

"Hi, Mom, I'm in space. What are you doing?"

"What do you mean you're in space? Where's your father?" she asked.

"I'm right here," Dad said leaning over so she could see his face.

"You're kidding, right?"

"I'm happy to report, madam, that your two fellows are officially astronauts and are safely orbiting the blue marble as we speak."

"What are you doing in space!"

"It's fine, Mom. It's the most amazing thing I've ever seen. Sir Robert's ship is so comfortable you wouldn't even believe it's a spaceship."

"I wish you would have called to let me know before deciding to blast off."

"It all happened so fast," Dad said. "It seemed like the opportunity of a lifetime."

"I'll have them safely back on the ground in less than twenty minutes, Mum."

I thought it was a little odd that he called Mom, Mum. I could tell by the look on her face that she didn't like it. "All right, but you call me the second you're back on Earth!" Mom insisted.

"Roger that," I said, hanging up.

"You were wondering about zero gravity," Sir Robert reminded me. "Press the button on your touch pad."

A clickable button appeared on my touch pad that read Zero Gravity. I pressed the button and immediately the glass cover above our heads rose up. It stretched up about fifteen feet before stopping.

Sir Robert unclicked his harness and rolled forward into zero gravity. "Feel free to unbuckle when you're ready."

"Let's go!" Dad said enthusiastically.

I clicked the button on my harness and immediately felt weightless. Rather than stay in my seat like I would have on Earth, I gently floated out. I reached out to grab something to balance myself and ended up grabbing Dad's ankle. Sir Robert was already about five feet above us and doing somersaults. I noticed a pen fall out of his pocket and float in the air near him.

I pushed off Dad's ankle and propelled up toward the ceiling of the ship. I tucked my knees up to my chest and rotated over in a flip. "This is the absolute best thing ever! We've got to get Mom up here one day," I said.

"You can e-mail her a video of the entire flight. The ship records everything," Sir Robert said.

"Can I have a copy?" I asked.

"If your plan to capture the asteroid works, you can have more than that," he said.

For the first time since I climbed into the ship, I thought about the real reason we'd come to the desert. We were there to help capture an asteroid. It was time to return to Earth and get to work. Sir Robert clicked a button and the ceiling started lowering back to its original size. We all buckled back in and began our descent to Earth. I took one last look at the planet from space.

"Soak it up, Benji," Dad said. "You may never get an opportunity to visit space again."

"I'm quite certain this is the first of many space flights for young Master Franklin," Sir Robert said.

"I hope you're right," I said.

"Trust me," he said. "You'll be back."

CHAPTER 19

Nice Catch!

It was a good thing that we got an early start on all the preparations because the asteroid was traveling faster than we originally realized. After about a week of people working around the clock at the facility we were ready to put my plan into motion. Dad and I stayed in New Mexico the whole week. Since we were working, Mom decided to stay and help out in Shiny Desert until we were ready to head home.

Dad, Sir Robert, and I went back into space in one of his ships before the rockets were launched. One of his teams stayed at the facility and another prepared the landing spot for the asteroid. Once we were in space Sir Robert handed me the digital screen that controlled the rockets. "The moment of truth has arrived, Benji."

I took a deep breath. There was so much adrenaline rushing through my body I felt like I might burst. "What if this doesn't work?" I asked.

"What if it does?" he said.

"It will be the most amazing thing ever," I said.

"Then let's do the most amazing thing ever!"

Dad patted me on the back. "Let's do it. It's time to put things in motion."

On my screen I had a view of the asteroid. It was approaching exactly as we'd planned. I clicked the button to launch the first four rockets. The video from the ground showed all four firing and launching. I waited a few seconds and clicked to launch the fifth rocket containing the graphene mesh. It blasted off exactly as planned.

"Phase one complete," Sir Robert said.

We watched the video screens from each rocket and the coordinates of where they were located. Within minutes, they were in place.

They were each programmed to carry out the mission, but if anything went wrong, I had the ability to override the program from our ship.

The fifth rocket released the graphene mesh and cut its engines as planned. The other four maneuvered into position. Each one docked into a corner of the mesh, spreading it out like a gigantic space web. We zoomed closer in our ship for a visual inspection of the setup. I felt like I was dreaming. There I was in space about to catch an asteroid!

"Is this really happening?" I asked Dad as we circled the mesh.

"It is really happening," Dad said. "Don't ask me how, but it's happening!"

"We better move to a safer distance," Sir Robert said. "This is all going to happen very fast."

We traveled for a while until we all agreed we were safely away from the asteroid. We tracked its every move on the video screen.

It was moving so fast I started to feel concerned that it would destroy the mesh and crash to Earth. I held my breath for what seemed like forever as it approached.

Closer...closer...

It made a direct hit with the center of the mesh, which ignited all four rockets. The force of the rockets pulled in the opposite direction that the asteroid was traveling. We worried that the force of the asteroid would tear the mesh away from the rockets, but the graphene was strong enough to hold on. It stretched out a bunch, and kept stretching!

The force of the rockets slowed the asteroid dramatically. The force of the asteroid's speed and the force of the rockets created an epic battle of tug-of-war. Which would win?

Within a few minutes it was over and the asteroid was gliding safely under the control of the rockets. "Phase two complete," Sir Robert said sounding relieved.

Dad didn't say a word. He was sweating pretty heavily. I noticed that his fingers were crossed. "Are you all right, Dad?" I asked.

"About as good as I can be under the circumstances."

Phase three of the plan was the part I was looking forward to most. The rockets carefully guided the asteroid down toward Earth. We followed behind. We were close enough to watch it with our own eyes. The asteroid was far more massive than I'd imagined. It was like a floating mountain.

I couldn't believe how well the rockets were working. At the pace they were going we'd be on the surface in a matter of minutes.

"You should probably call Mom," Dad said.

He was right.

I clicked the screen and dialed Mom. Her face appeared on the screen. "Hi, Mom! What are you doing?"

"I'm working. We just got back to Shiny Desert a little while ago. I made another run back to the farm to pick up more supplies for the town."

"Great! Do me a favor. Head outside and look up in the sky."

"Benji, I'm pretty busy. We've got a load of supplies that we need to organize."

"Trust me. I'll see you in a few minutes." Then I hung up.

"Phase four coming up," Dad said.

"Phase four on the way," I said. We were getting low enough that I could see the ground. We were under the clouds. Things were coming into view.

"There," Dad said. "There's Mom's truck."

I saw the truck and spotted Mom. She had walked out of a building and was looking up at us. I could only imagine what was going through her mind gazing up at a massive asteroid supported by four rockets.

People from the nearby town were pouring out of the buildings too. There was a real commotion.

The rockets safely landed the asteroid on the exact coordinates we'd programmed. It was the perfect spot just outside the town.

The ground vibrated when the space rock made contact. Sir Robert landed our ship near the asteroid and Mom ran over to meet us.

CHAPTER 20
Bright Future

By the time the team sprayed down the asteroid with water and it cooled to a safe level, hundreds of people had lined up for a look. Sir Robert's team handed him a microphone.

"Citizens of Shiny Desert," he began. "We at Dransling Industries realize that you've fallen on hard times. You're a hard-working community. You don't deserve the misfortune that fell upon you when Techron left you without jobs. I wasn't familiar with your story until a young friend of mine brought it to my attention. Through a series of miraculous events we've managed to save the planet from a deadly asteroid *and* your town all at once.

"Please accept this asteroid as a gift. It should provide adequate income as a tourist destination for many years to come."

"Additionally," said the billionaire. "I plan to move a portion of my business here to your town. I'm building my space tourism business, and I'm opening an assembly plant right here in Shiny Desert. Construction of the new plant will begin as soon as possible and we will begin hiring tomorrow. We look forward to a bright future together!"

The crowd cheered.

"This was all your idea, wasn't it?" Mom asked. "I don't know what to say. Benji, you managed to solve the town's problems and save the planet in one swoop. You're my very own pint-sized hero!"

I was kind of overwhelmed by it all. It had been a crazy couple of weeks. I knew my life would never be the same again, but I also knew I wanted to try to keep from changing as much as I could.

That's when I heard Sir Robert say, "Folks, I can't stand up here and take all the credit for today. There's a young man who was the brains behind this whole thing. He's here somewhere..."

"He's talking about you, Benji," Mom said. "Get ready to go up on the stage."

I took Mom by the hand and quickly led her out of the crowd. "What are we doing?" Mom asked.

"The hero never sticks around for a thank-you," I reminded her. "Besides, I have something I want to show you."

I led Mom over to the ship. "Get a load of this!" I exclaimed.

"Benji, this is very pretty, but we should be getting back."

"I'd rather show you something else," I said.

Dad ran up to us. "I lost you guys back there. Benji, Sir Robert is looking for you."

"Let him take the credit. I'd rather take Mom for a spin."

"Great idea," Dad said. He opened the door. "After you, my dear."

"Where are we going?" Mom asked.

"Trust me," I said. We all climbed in. I called Sir Robert's phone. His face appeared on the screen. "Benji, where are you? These people want to thank you."

"You enjoy it. I'm going to take my Mom for a spin if that's all right with you."

"By all means. Just don't forget to swing by and pick me up when you're done."

"Will do," I said. I hung up and told Mom to get ready.

"Benji, do you know how to control this thing?"

"I don't need to. It's already programmed."

"Programmed to go where?"

"To space," I said, pressing the launch button. The ship lifted off the ground. Mom screamed and grabbed onto Dad.

"Will I like it?" she asked, looking terrified.

"You'll love it," I said, and the ship bolted up toward outer space.

Mom let out another scream, and then she said, "Benji, you're too much! What on Earth are you going to accomplish next!"

"I have no idea," I said. "But I can't wait to find out!"

NOTICE OF PAYMENT

FROM:
NEO (Near Earth Object)

TO:
Benjamin "Benji" Franklin

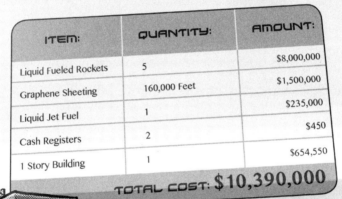

ITEM:	QUANTITY:	AMOUNT:
Liquid Fueled Rockets	5	$8,000,000
Graphene Sheeting	160,000 Feet	$1,500,000
Liquid Jet Fuel	1	$235,000
Cash Registers	2	$450
1 Story Building	1	$654,550
TOTAL COST:		$10,390,000

PAYMENT DUE UPON RECEIPT

PAID!

Cha-Ching!!

RAYMOND BEAN

Raymond Bean is the best-selling author of the Sweet Farts and School Is A Nightmare series. His books have ranked #1 in Children's Humor, Humorous Series, and Fantasy and Adventure categories. He writes for kids that claim they don't like reading.

Mr. Bean is a fourth grade teacher with fifteen years of classroom experience. He lives with his wife and two children in New York.